Illustrated Classics

DRACULA

Om KIDZ
An imprint of Om Books International

In the late 19th century, a young English lawyer called Jonathan Harker travelled to Castle Dracula, in Transylvania, Eastern Europe. He had to conclude a real estate transaction with a nobleman named Count Dracula.

Local peasants warned Harker against going to the sinister castle. They gave him crucifixes and other charms to ward off evil.

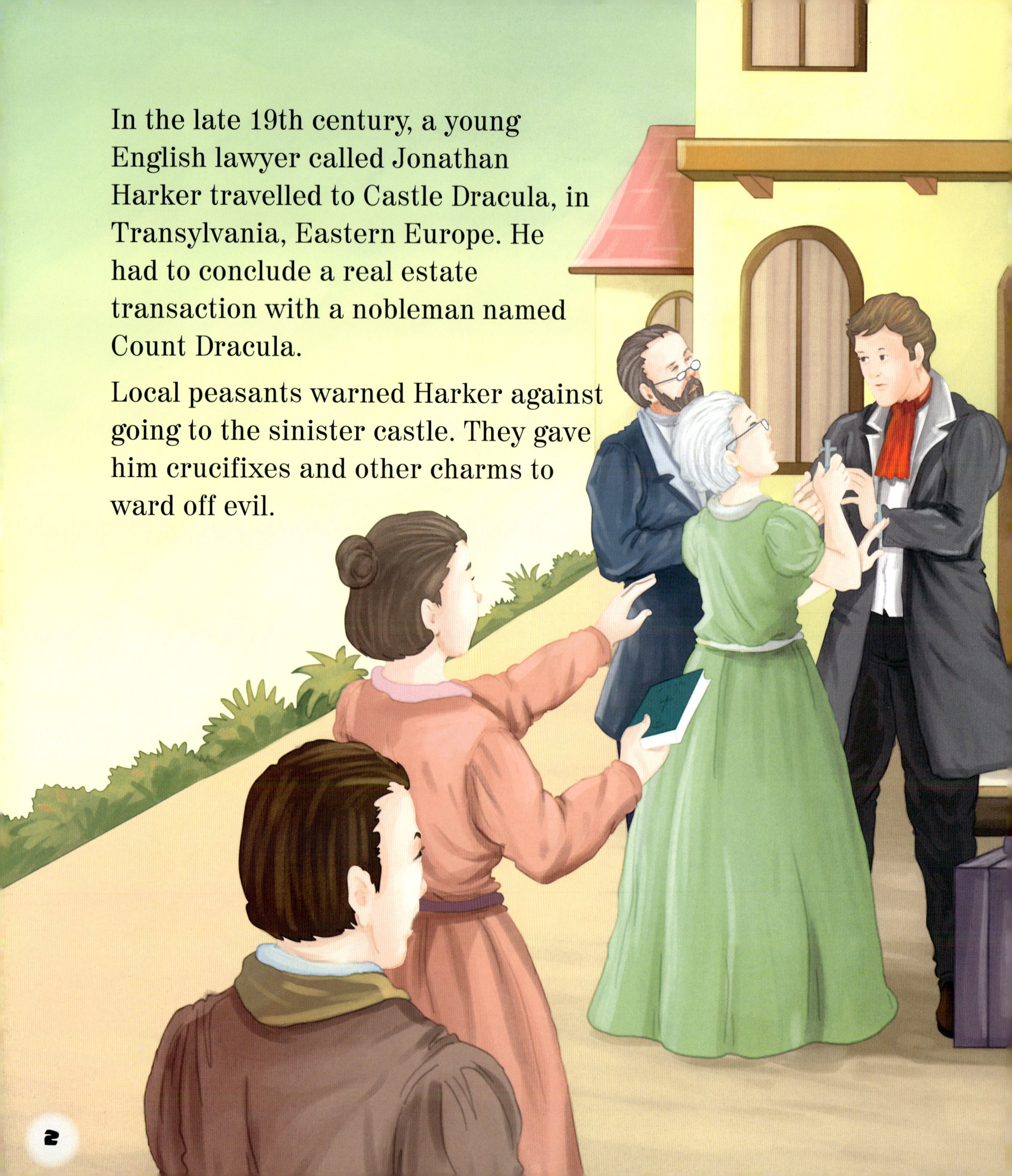

Scared but determined, Harker boarded the Count's carriage that had been sent to fetch him. The journey to the castle was frightening, with angry wolves attacking the carriage on the way.

Harker arrived at the castle to discover that the elderly Dracula was a well-educated, hospitable gentleman. But a few days later, when Harker accidentally cut himself while shaving, the Count lunged furiously at his throat. Harker discovered the Count's dark secret—he survived by drinking the blood of humans.

One evening, Harker was attacked by three beautiful female vampires. But the Count drove them away, saying that Harker belonged to him.

The Count escaped Harker's attempt to kill him, and left for England with fifty boxes of earth. A weak and sick Harker was left behind, a prisoner in the castle.

Meanwhile, in England, Harker's fiancée, Mina Murray, received news from her friend, Lucy Westenra. Lucy had decided to marry a man named Arthur Holmwood.

Mina visited Lucy at the seaside town of Whitby. A few days later, they spotted a wrecked Russian ship. The crew was missing and the captain dead. The sole living member on this ship was a large dog that ran ashore and disappeared into the countryside. The only cargo found on the ship was fifty boxes of earth from Count Dracula.

Soon after, Lucy began sleepwalking. One night, Mina discovered Lucy in the town cemetery. Mina saw a dark form with glowing red eyes bend over Lucy. Lucy became ill and pale, with two tiny red marks on her throat. Dr. Seward called for his old mentor, Professor Van Helsing, as he was unable to diagnose the illness.

Meanwhile, Harker, who was suffering from brain fever, escaped from the castle and travelled to Budapest, where Mina joined him. Van Helsing arrived in Whitby and examined Lucy. He ordered that Lucy's chambers be covered with garlic, a traditional method for warding off vampires. Lucy began to recover, until one day, her mother unknowingly removed all the garlic from her room.

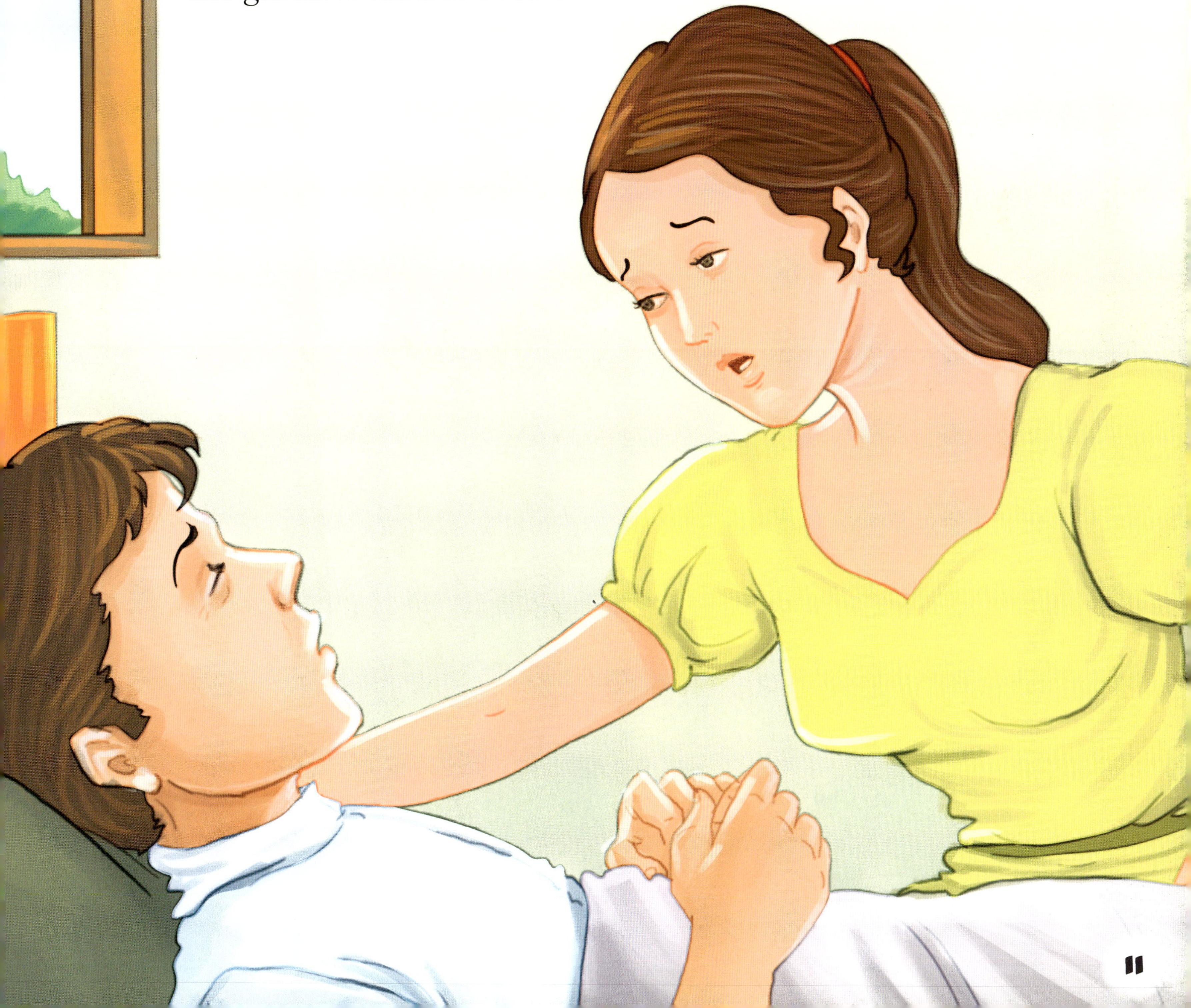

One night, a wolf broke into Lucy's house and attacked her. Lucy's mother suffered a heart attack and died. Lucy was killed by the wolf.

Van Helsing led Holmwood, Seward and Quincy Morris to Lucy's tomb. He convinced them that Lucy had been converted into a vampire. The men didn't believe him till they saw Lucy attack a small child.

That's when they decided to perform the vampire killing ritual to put Lucy's soul to rest. When the undead Lucy slept, Holmwood drove a stake through her heart. Then her head was cut off and her mouth stuffed with garlic.

The men took an oath to destroy Count Dracula.

Mina and Harker got married and returned to England to join the anti-Dracula squad. The team tracked down the boxes of earth that Dracula used as a sanctuary. But one of Dr. Seward's mental patients let Dracula into Dr. Seward's asylum. The Count attacked Mina and slowly, she began transforming into a vampire. The men destroyed all the boxes of earth, except one, in which Dracula escaped to Transylvania.

The men chased him, dividing their forces across land and sea. Reaching earlier, they killed the three female vampires in Dracula's castle and sealed the entrances with holy objects. A band of gypsies brought Dracula in the box to the castle. The men overpowered the gypsies and found Dracula sleeping in the box. Harker cut off the vampire's head and Morris drove his knife deep into the Count's heart. Count Dracula crumbled to dust!

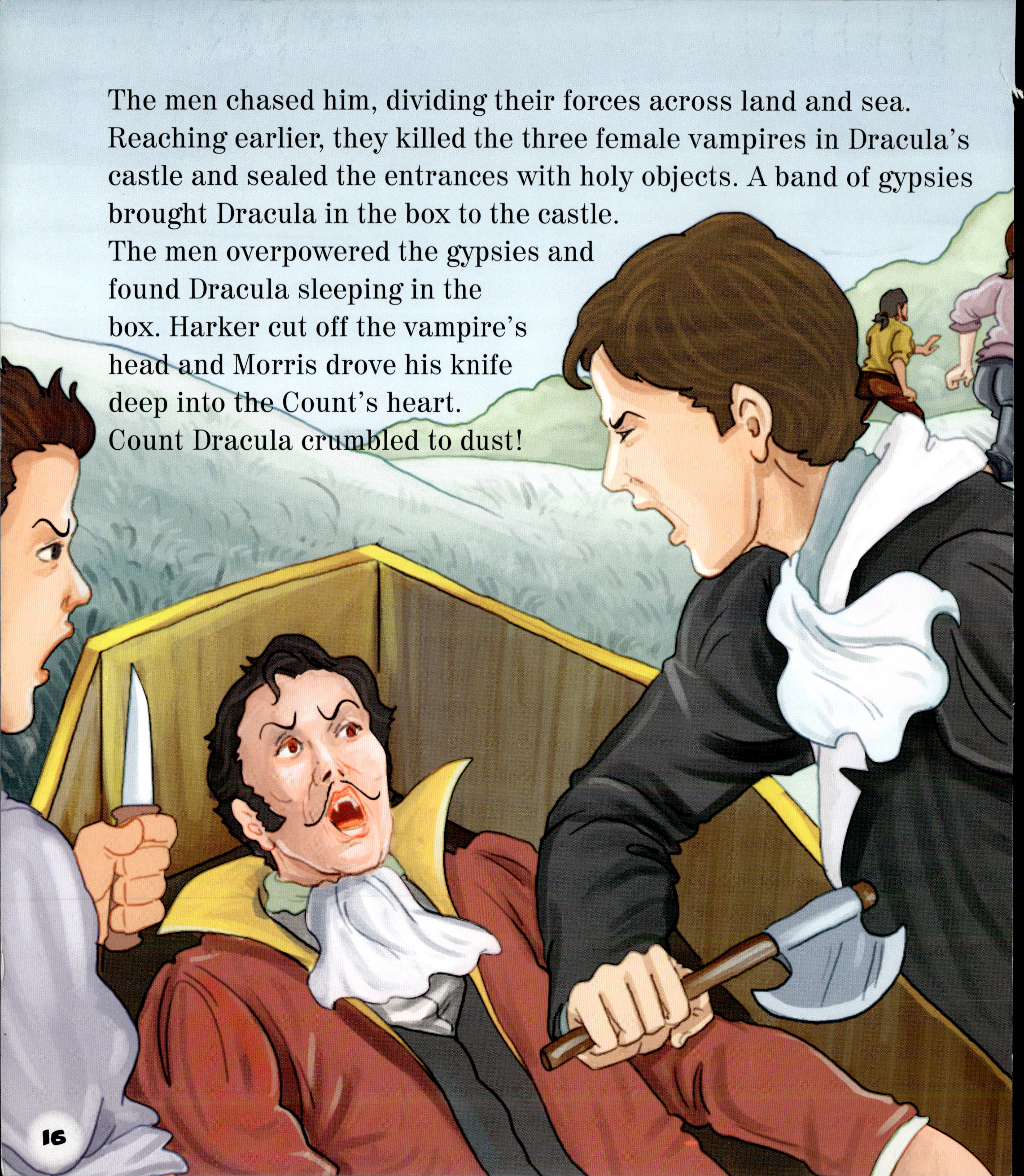